WOOF

THE RUNAWAY
ROBOT

Check out more Wednesday and Woof mysteries!

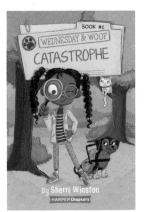

HARPERChapters

BOOK #3

WEDNESDAY & WOOF

THE RUNAWAY ROBOT

By **SHERRI WINSTON**

Illustrated by
GLADYS JOSE

HARPER
An Imprint of HarperCollinsPublishers

TO MY LAUREN, YOU MADE ME A BETTER
PERSON. I WILL ALWAYS LOVE YOU, DEAR
DAUGHTER. YOU ARE MISSED. ♥

Wednesday and Woof #3: The Runaway Robot
Copyright © 2022 by HarperCollins Publishers
All rights reserved. Manufactured in Italy.
No part of this book may be used or reproduced in any manner
whatsoever without written permission except in the case of brief
quotations embodied in critical articles and reviews. For information
address HarperCollins Children's Books, a division of HarperCollins
Publishers, 195 Broadway, New York, NY 10007.
www.harperchapters.com

Library of Congress Control Number: 2021951499
ISBN 978-0-06-297610-9 — ISBN 978-0-06-297609-3 (pbk.)

Typography by Catherine Lee and Alice Wang
22 23 24 25 26   RTLO   10 9 8 7 6 5 4 3 2 1

First Edition

TABLE of CONTENTS

From *The Big Book of Detective Tips:*

How to come up with Ideas:

1. Return to the scene of the crime.

2. Ask yourself, "How could this happen?"

3. Imagine the possibilities.

CHAPTER #1

ROBOT ON THE LOOSE!

ZOOM!

A robot dog shoots across the shiny wood floor of room 12. It makes a *whir-whir-whir* sound. Bottle caps jingle around its neck like a collar.

Then comes another sound:

"Help!" cries Anita B. Moosier. She is my bossy neighbor and also my second grade classmate. "Rin Tin Robot is getting away!"

I look at my best friend, Belinda Bundy. She looks at me. My dog, Woof, looks at me, too. He is not a robot. He is a support dog. He comes to school because of my juvenile arthritis. He says, "Woof!"

"That's right, Woof! We have to help!" I say.

"We can't let the robot dog escape!" says Belinda Bundy, ready for action.

Quickly, Woof dashes to block its path. But before Rin Tin Robot reaches him, it hits a cushion on the rug. Then it spins off in another direction!

"That way!" I point.

"Woof!" says my dog.

"Oh my word!" says our teacher, Mrs. Gubbins.

When the robot flies directly toward her, she bends to try and catch it, but Rin Tin Robot is too fast. It races away! *Ziiiiiiiiip!*

"Anita B., what did you do to that thing?" says Calvin. "Or should I say . . . what did your *parents* do?"

"What is that supposed to mean, Calvin T. Parker?" says Anita B. "My dad helped, but I built it myself. And anyway, mind your own business."

Woof races past the robot and skids to a

stop. He waits until Rin Tin Robot rolls right into him. Then Woof curves his body so the robot has no place to go!

Belinda Bundy cheers. "That's what I call teamwork. The Wednesday and Woof Detective Agency saves the day again!"

Anita B. scoops up her runaway robot. "We didn't need any Detective Walia," she mutters.

Sigh! "My name is Wednesday Walia Nadir, Anita B. Moose-Pickles, and you know it!" I tell her. Everybody calls me Walia unless I'm solving a case, and then they use my professional name—Wednesday. "And you're sooooo welcome for us helping you!"

"Woof!" agrees my dog. I rest against him. My juvenile arthritis makes my body feel tired sometimes. So does Anita B.

She puts a hand on her hip and says, "And *my* name is Moosier. Moose-E-A. It's French!"

It's annoying, if you ask me.

Calvin cuts in. "Well, now that we've finished roll call, you should know I made my *own* robot. *All by myself.* And *I'm* going to win the science fair, not you, Anita B.!" Ever since that time Calvin thought she stole a drone, he and Anita B. haven't been so friendly.

6

On the wall in room 12, there is a poster about the scientific method. There is also a long banner that says:

LOWER GRADES SCIENCE FAIR
Thursday Night
in the Gym
First Prize: a trophy
and a $20 gift card

Everyone in my class has made a robot for this science fair.

"I don't care if I win or not," I whisper to Belinda Bundy.

"Me either," she whispers back. "I love my Bunny Bot."

"And I love my Inspector Robot," I say. "He has a hidden camera in his belly."

Jack, who likes to make *zoom-zoom* noises, looks at Rin Tin Robot and says, "That's pretty cool." He turns to Calvin and announces, "I know you wanted to win because of your brother and all, but I think Anita B. has you beat."

Calvin snarls. "Oh yeah? We'll see about that!"

ZOOM-ZOOM! YOU'VE ALREADY READ 622 WORDS! WAY TO GO!

CHAPTER #2

SNOWBALL FIGHT!

I GIVE Calvin a curious look. Detectives are always curious.

Belinda Bundy and I move closer to him, so no one else can hear. Belinda Bundy says, "Calvin, it's okay if you win or don't win, as long as you like your robot."

"Yeah," I say, "you don't have to win just because your brother won last year."

Our voices are soft and gentle. Still, he flinches like we've pinched him.

"He beats me in everything. I have to win, okay?" he snaps.

Jack rolls his red toy sports car down the swoopy arm of the reading sofa. He asks Anita B., "How did you make Rin Tin Robot go so fast?"

"With springs and fast wheels!" she says. She shows how it's made of different-sized tin cans. Then she turns Rin Tin Robot

upside down. "Under here I have a piece of thick cardboard. I added springs here and gave my robot wheels from an old toy truck of mine, and then . . ."

"*Zoom-zoom!*" says Jack.

Anita B. nods. "There's even room inside the can for storage!"

The dog's body is hollow. Anita B. has an empty toilet paper roll stashed inside. She takes it out and peeks through one end and everyone laughs.

Except for Calvin. He is sulking.

Calvin says, "*I* made a robotic truck named Rover. He can pick up bottle caps *and* toilet paper rolls. My brother thinks he's so smart, but he's not the best at everything!"

Calvin's brother, Carter, is in fourth grade. He is very smart. One day, on the sidewalk, he told me:

"Step on a crack, break your mama's back!"

I never would've known. I avoid cracks when I can now, just in case he's right. Anyway, Calvin sometimes competes with Carter even when Carter doesn't know they're competing. Lucky for him, Carter is in the upper grades science fair this year.

We all press closer to see Calvin's robot. It looks very complicated.

14

Jack shakes his head. He says, "It's nice, man, but my money is on that crazy tin-can dog!"

Then Mrs. Gubbins joins us. "I'm glad you got your robot under control, Anita B. Now, please take Rin Tin Robot to your desk. I need Walia and Belinda to return to the class pets. They need their morning routine, girls," she says.

Me and Belinda Bundy give fresh water, hay, and a

few slivers of carrot to Cookie and Crackers, the two cute hamsters that are our class pets. Their playpen sits on top of the bookshelves in the center of the room.

"Look, Crackers is hiding in the corner! He loves to hide!" Belinda Bundy says. She loves animals and plans to be a bunny when she grows up.

She adds, "I've never seen Calvin so worked up."

Woof, sitting by my leg, thumps his tail in agreement. Woof notices things about people. That's why he's such a good detective's assistant.

"I know," I say. "Why he needs to beat his brother so bad is a mystery even I can't solve."

Belinda turns and calls out, "Anita B., may we use some of your toilet paper rolls for the hamsters? I want to build them a tunnel."

Anita B. shrugs, so Belinda Bundy bounces over, takes a few of the empty cardboard tubes, and places them inside the playpen. (Belinda Bundy often hops like a bunny.)

"Look at Cookie and Crackers!" she says.

Their noses twitch close together. "They look like they are sharing a secret!"

I giggle. We watch little Crackers climb into one of the toilet paper rolls.

"They're playing hide-and-seek!" says Belinda Bundy.

We are almost finished with Cookie and Crackers when Mrs. Gubbins gets everyone's attention.

"Boys and girls, this is a very special afternoon. We've been challenged to a snowball fight by Mr. Fussbudget's class!" she says.

"YAY!" the students in room 12 shout all at once. We all go into superspeed to get outside.

We place our robots on the bookshelf, we get our coats, and we race for the door! Everyone except Calvin, that is. He doesn't get his coat. He turns left when the rest of us turn right.

Outside, my twin brother, Raafe, and the rest of Mr. Fussbudget's class are waiting. "Walia, your class is going down!" he yells. I grin and—*SMACK!*—throw a snowball

right into his middle.

Snowballs fly everywhere. Someone gets me in the knee! When the battle ends, Woof and I are out of breath. Then Mrs. Gubbins declares our class the winners!

"We're number one!" chant the students of room 12. "We're number one!"

Our faces are cold, and our mittens are wet, but we are happy.

23

When we go inside, I notice that our classroom door is slightly open.

Mrs. Gubbins sees it, too. "Hmm . . . ," she says. "What's going on here?"

Kids rush through the open door. They begin taking off their coats and gloves and boots and hats. Then there is a loud noise.

"HELP!" shrieks Anita B. "Rin Tin Robot—he's gone!"

CHAPTER #3

INVESTIGATION STATION

"HE WAS right here, wasn't he, Walia?" Anita B. sniffs. Is she crying?

Mrs. Gubbins looks at me and Woof and Belinda Bundy. We nod.

Just then, Calvin comes back into the room. Belinda Bundy says, "Calvin, you were pretty upset about Anita B.'s robot being so fast. Did you—"

"No!" he says, cutting her off.

But Anita B. points a finger at him.

"That's right! He was being mean and saying he had to win and boys were better than girls and he was going to crush Rin Tin Robot!" she says.

"Um, I don't think Calvin said that," I say.

"He stole it! I know he did!" Anita B. insists.

"Class, class, I want everyone to take their seats. I need you to work on your posters for the science fair," says Mrs. Gubbins. She turns to face me and Belinda Bundy. "Girls, can you two search for her robot? Anita B., you come with me."

"Wait!" Anita B. says. She digs into her pocket and pulls out a small, shiny object. It's a gold pin. "See? It's shaped like a tiny magnifying glass. Like a detective uses. You can have it, Walia Nadir, if you find Rin Tin Robot."

"Woof!" agrees my dog. He's always eager for a case.

I take the pin in my hand. It looks so cool.

But a funny feeling, like a slippery lump, fills my belly as I pass the pin back to Anita B. Everyone in the whole world—at least, the world of room 12—is looking at me.

"Belinda, I'll let you borrow the pin if you help," I say quickly. But she shakes her head.

"I'll help, but everybody knows *you're* the detective," she says.

That slippery feeling gets slipperier. Everyone expects me to solve this mystery. But what if I can't?

"Hrrrmph!" says Woof. See, he knows what I'm thinking even when I'm just thinking it. I run my fingers across the top of his head. He looks up, and I know he understands.

Belinda whispers, "Actually, I'm pretty sure Calvin didn't do it. I just remembered he goes to the nurse's office to get his breathing treatments. Same time every day."

I nod. I'd forgotten about his daily trip to the nurse. I smile at Calvin to make him feel better, but he looks mad—the kind of mad a kid feels when he's been wrongly accused.

"Anita B.," says Mrs. Gubbins, "will you help me prepare some hot cocoa while everyone gets to work?" The hot cocoa is the prize for our snowball fight victory!

"Okay," says Anita B. Her head drops down as she walks away.

Around the room, most kids are working on their posters. Me and Belinda start trying to crack the case!

We check cubbies and shelves. We search under the sofa with the swoopy arms and the book tree that holds Mrs. Gubbins's favorite books.

Belinda hop-hop-hops as we check beneath everyone's seats. Then we look around the corner by the sinks. We look *everywhere*. But there is no sign of Rin Tin Robot. The slippery feeling slides back into my belly.

When Anita B. looks at me, I shake my head. Her eyes get watery again. I'm used to Anita B. being bossy and mean—but crying? Nobody wants that!

"I need my detective book," I say softly. "Go get it, boy!"

32

Woof understands me right away. He goes to my cubby and returns carrying *The Big Book of Detective Tips*.

I flip the pages, looking for ideas.

CHAPTER THREE

De-mystifying 'de' mystery!

When a detective is trying to unearth clues, there are three simple rules to follow:

1. Study the scene.
2. Look for anything unusual.
3. Make some connections.

I shut my eyes and take a picture with my memory. It's room 12, exactly how it looked before the snowball fight. Everyone placing their robots on the shelf. Me and Belinda Bundy closing the hamsters into their playpen.

I remember how everyone was in a hurry. I remember how excited we were.

My brain is still working through the memories when there is another cry, more desperate than Anita B's. This time, it's Belinda Bundy!

"Oh no!" she says. Her eyes are huge. "Crackers is missing!"

CHAPTER #4
COOKIE BUT NO CRACKERS!

IS ROOM 12 having a crime wave?

Belinda Bundy takes a deep breath. She says, "Okay, let's look inside the pen some more. Crackers loves to hide."

Mrs. Gubbins comes over and peeks inside, too. There is Cookie, but no Crackers. Everyone in the classroom has questions on their faces.

And all those faces are looking at me for answers.

Belinda Bundy shakes her head. "He's not in there!" she says. She scoops up Cookie. "Poor Mr. Cookie, don't be sad. We'll find your best friend."

She nuzzles Cookie and listens as the tiny pet makes a *wheek-wheek-wheek* sound. She nods like she understands. Then she puts the squirmy hamster back inside the pen.

"Well, this is quite a pickle," Mrs. Gub-bins says. "We have a double mystery on our hands. Everyone, check carefully beneath your desks, and stay alert. I'm going to check next door with Mr. Fussbudget's class. Maybe they saw or heard something."

When she goes to the door between our classrooms, I squint. There is a whole new

mystery to take in. I'll need all my detecting skills to handle this.

Lucy Shelley, who made an alien robot, says, "Maybe a spaceship came down and beamed Crackers up to another planet."

Jack says, "Maybe a giant bird flew in and took the shiny pieces of the robot away. Along with Crackers! *Zooooooom!*"

"Woof!" says my dog. I can tell he thinks they're wrong. I agree.

But what *did* happen? Is there a connection between the two mysteries?

"I was so excited about the snowball fight," Belinda Bundy says, "maybe I didn't close the latch on the pen's door. I should have been more careful." Her face droops. Now she's feeling sad, too.

"Don't worry, Belinda Bundy," I say. "We'll find Crackers." She tries to smile, but her

face is only pretending.

"It's all my fault," she says as she walks away. She doesn't even hop. When Belinda Bundy stops hopping, things are serious.

What am I going to do? How can I help Belinda Bundy? I think, think, think about what my book says. What am I missing? I know one thing for sure. I need some good ideas.

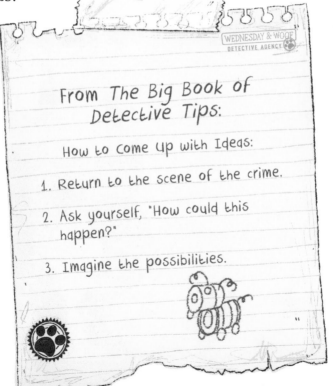

From *The Big Book of Detective Tips*:

How to Come Up with Ideas:

1. Return to the scene of the crime.

2. Ask yourself, "How could this happen?"

3. Imagine the possibilities.

Mrs. Gubbins returns with Mr. Fussbud-get. He is soft and round, with glasses and a circle of hair on top of his head. He always walks very fast. And talks fast, too.

"What's going on here? What's happening? That poor hamster—lost! What a disaster!"

he says, taking
a lap around
our classroom
and flapping
his arms.
Mom calls
that "panic
mode." I
call it funny
to look at.

Raafe pokes
his head into
our room.

He says, "Mr. Fussbudget, we all looked. Nobody has found Crackers yet."

"Thank you, Raafe," Mrs. Gubbins says. She turns to me and says, "Walia, do you have any ideas?"

I chew my lip. I lean against Woof a little. A tiny ache pulses in my wrist. Stress does that sometimes to my JA.

"Woof!" says my dog.

"You're right, Woof. I need to just take a deep breath and blow the stress out," I say.

I feel better after I do that. At least, until Mr. Fussbudget starts yelling again.

"We can't trust this mystery to a child!" says Mr. Fussbudget. He is really frazzled. He throws his arms up in the air. "A hamster lost on the eve of the science fair. Disaster!

We must call someone. The principal. The security guard. The FBI!"

"Give my sister a chance, Mr. Fussbudget," Raafe says. "She's really good at solving mysteries!"

It feels good to know Raafe believes in me. Belinda Bundy moves over and squeezes my hand, and that makes me feel better, too.

Then I ask myself: *Are there two mysteries here . . . or one?*

I tug Woof's harness and we return to the bookshelf. When I touch the latch on the hamster pen, it pops right open. But it shouldn't open so easily!

If Crackers leaned against it, he could have opened the door himself.

Then something else pops into my head.

"Anita B.'s robot was sitting right here," I say. "Right next to the hamster pen."

"Woof!" says my dog. *Thump-thump* goes his tail. Woof thinks we're onto something.

I imagine more possibilities. Then a smile begins to spread across my face.

A DOUBLE MYSTERY?! HOW DO YOU THINK THE MYSTERIES CONNECT?

"LOOK AT this," I say. I show my classmates the important clue. "The latch to the hamsters' cage doesn't close properly. That means Belinda Bundy didn't have to *leave* it open. Crackers could have *pushed* it open."

Pointing to the wall poster, I say, "All we have to do is apply the steps."

Calvin says, "Of the scientific method?"

I nod. "We can use science to help us solve the mystery!"

THE SCIENTIFIC METHOD

The Steps to the
Scientific Method Are:

1. Ask a question.

2. Make a hypothesis.

3. Test the hypothesis
   with an experiment.

4. Draw a conclusion.

5. Communicate
   the results.

"Well," says Calvin, "the first step is to start with a question."

"Yeah!" says Anita B. "So, what's the question?"

Belinda Bundy tilts her head and looks at the pen. "How?" she says. "That's the question. *How* could sweet little Crackers just . . . disappear?"

"Exactly!" I say. "So, if the question is 'how,' the next step is to make a hypothesis." That's where imagination and science come together.

I tell everyone my hypothesis: "If Crackers got out of the cage because the latch wasn't closed, he could have climbed into the toilet paper tube inside Rin Tin Robot's stomach!"

"Crackers loved to hide in the tunnel that we made!" Belinda Bundy points out.

The next step is to test the hypothesis. Luckily, Mrs. Gubbins has some empty tin cans under the sink. We borrow a toilet paper roll from Anita B.'s stash and lay it inside an empty tin can.

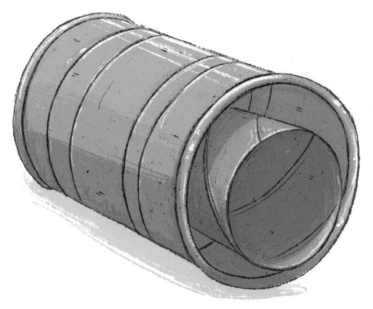

"Belinda Bundy, I need your help," I say. She nods.

"Woof!" says my dog. He moves around to my other side. I'm sure glad no one in Mrs. Gubbins's class is allergic to my detective's assistant. I don't know what I'd do without Woof.

Calvin pushes a stool up to the bookshelf so I can sit. Since he's my brother's best friend, he understands my JA.

"Thanks, Calvin," I say.

"What is this going to prove?" Anita B. huffs.

"Just a second," I say. I look at Belinda Bundy and say, "Set him free, please."

Belinda Bundy says, "Run free, little Cookie," and the fluffy creature sniffs his way across the top of the shelf. He heads right to the can. In less than a minute, he

climbs inside it and snuggles into the toilet paper roll! When he wiggles, the can rolls, and Belinda Bundy catches it in her hand.

Everyone applauds. "Yay!" they shout. Everyone except Anita B.

"So Crackers stole my robot? Why does everything always happen to me?" she whines.

Belinda Bundy shakes her head. "Crackers didn't steal your robot. Hamsters can't think like that. It's just that the robot was nearby and easy to get into."

"Right!" I say. "That's our conclusion."

"Okay," says Jack, "then what?"

"Yeah, then what?" Anita B. says with a scowl.

"Woof! Woof!" says my dog. Woof always has my back.

"Now that we've gone through the scientific method, it's clear. Crackers has to be joyriding in Rin Tin Robot," I say. "The only question now is, where did they go?"

"Um, Wednesday," says Belinda Bundy as she hop-hop-hops over to me. "I know how we can figure out where they went."

She taps my robot and says, "I think Inspector Robot is exactly what we need!"

CHAPTER #6
PICTURE THIS!

ANITA B. glares at me. "Are you *sure* Calvin didn't do it?" she asks.

"No, Anita B., I did not!" says Calvin, fists on his hips. "You're just mad because I made my robot all by myself and your dad made yours *all by himself.*"

There is a gasp. Everyone, even Mr. Fussbudget, sucks in air. Anita B. puts one hand on her hip and narrows her eyes. She says, "Look, Mr. Big Mouth, your truck robot was built out of a kit. Mine is one hundred percent recycled stuff. The only things I bought were a few dollar-store toys so I could use their springs. So you better quit saying my daddy built my robot, buster, unless you want to find your precious kit bot smashed into a million pieces."

See, one thing you learn in the detective business is that people will surprise you. Who knew Anita B. would ever say something that would make me feel proud of her? The world is a funny place. Right, Woof?

He nods even though I didn't say a word. Like I said, Woof understands me.

Still, I don't want Anita B. smashing things. I say, "I think Belinda Bundy has a great idea. I'd completely forgotten about Inspector Robot."

"Who?" says Calvin.

"Walia's robot," Belinda Bundy says. "It's like a periscope with a tiny spy camera inside."

Instead of a tin can, my robot is made out of a milk carton and mirrors. There's a window up top on one side, and down below on the other side, with a mirror opposite each one.

"See these mirrors?" I say. "They reflect to the camera what's going on through the windows. When it senses motion, the camera records. If Crackers and Rin Tin Robot rolled past where it was pointing, I'm sure Inspector Robot recorded it."

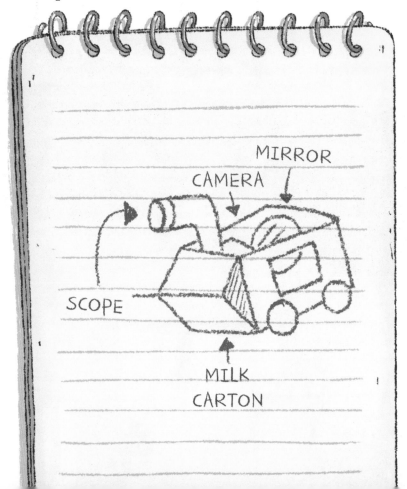

Grandpa loaned me his phone, which I can use to see all the video Inspector Robot records. Now I take the phone out of my cubby and power it up. Mrs. Gubbins, Mr. Fussbudget, and the rest of the class crowd around for a better view.

"Look at this!" I say.

Plain as day, we see Rin Tin Robot dashing out the door!

"Somehow the door was left open when we went outside," Belinda Bundy recaps. "Rin Tin Robot got out, and Crackers is hitching a ride."

Too bad we still don't know where he is.

"What are we going to do now?" asks Calvin.

A case of the nervous itches attacks my arms. I have to figure something out. And quickly.

"Woof!" says Woof. I know exactly what he means.

"To the hallway!" I say.

"Oh my!" says Mr. Fussbudget. "We can't have children roaming the hallways unattended. Who knows what might happen? Who knows?"

"Mr. Fussbudget is right," says Mrs. Gubbins. "We cannot all go. We might disturb the other classes."

"Aw, man!" the whole class says together. Mrs. Gubbins taps her chin with her finger.

I know this is her thinking face, because Mom has one just like it.

"Wednesday," Mrs. Gubbins begins, "why don't you and Belinda Bundy take Woof and *quietly* check along the corridor for the missing, uh, well, the missing robot and hamster."

"I want to come, too!" cries Anita B.

"Don't worry, Anita B.," I say. "I won't let you down. Come on, Belinda Bundy."

Woof trots along beside me. I hold on to his harness for support. My knees hurt a little, but I won't let that slow me down. Nothing's going to stop me now that I'm hot on the trail.

The hallway is a mysterious place when it's empty. You can almost hear the quiet bouncing off the hard floors and walls. At one end, the smooth floor dead-ends at the water fountain.

I notice something as we walk. "Hey, look

at this," I say, pointing at something on the ground. Woof uses his nose and teeth to scoop the thing up.

"A bottle cap?" asks Belinda Bundy.

I hold it up and examine it. "Remember? Rin Tin Robot had a collar made of bottle caps," I say.

"That's right!" Belinda Bundy says. "But where is sweet Crackers?"

"One mystery at a time," I tell her. "If we find the robot, we also find the hamster!"

ONLY TWO MORE CHAPTERS LEFT! WHERE DO YOU THINK THEY'LL FIND CRACKERS AND THE ROBOT?

CHAPTER #7

EXHIBIT
(HALL) A

WE FOLLOW two more bottle caps to the water fountain. Next to it, we find Liam Davis. He is a third grader on safety patrol. His teacher lets him sit in the halls during recess to make sure no one runs or pushes or gets too loud. Also, because he is allergic to just about everything outside.

"Achoo!" Liam sneezes as soon as we get closer. He says, "Sorry. I might be allergic to your dog." Woof steps back.

"Did you happen to see a tin-can robot race through here?" I ask.

He frowns. "No, but I wish I had. I get pretty bored sitting out here by myself."

When I ask if he has any idea where Rin Tin Robot might be, he thinks for a moment. He sneezes two times before saying, "Mrs. Tallyhoo has been turning the gym into an exhibit hall. Her class made tiny gardens. *Achoo!*"

The floor slopes downward toward the gym. I have to walk carefully because my legs feel weak. I grasp Woof's harness with one hand. Belinda Bundy reaches for my other hand.

We walk down the sloping floor, then Liam opens the gym door for us.

Inside, the gym has been turned into a whole new world. There are large poster boards explaining why eggs float or how weather works. I can see where our class will set up our robots!

"Anita's robot and Crackers could be any-where," says Belinda Bundy. She has lost some of her bounce. I squeeze her fingers to comfort her.

"I think we'll be able to narrow that down," I say.

Some of the displays are on tables covered in white cloths. The tiny gardens are in wooden trays lined up on the floor. Carefully, with Woof's help, I bend down to take a closer look at them.

"And now I'm pretty sure where Crackers went," I add.

Mrs. Tallyhoo comes over. "Do you children have permission to be here?" she asks.

We nod. "Yes, ma'am," I say. "And . . . where are your carrots?"

Belinda Bundy looks at me. I look at her. Before Mrs. Tallyhoo can answer, Woof sniffs around a garden tray at his feet. "Woof!" he barks. I look where he is looking and see a row of fluffy green leaves that look like a soft green Afro standing out of the dirt!

"Carrots," I say with a grin.

"Crackers loves carrots!" says Belinda Bundy. "Just like a bunny!"

In the soil, which smells like rainy days in spring, sits a tin-can robot. Belinda Bundy reaches over and plucks it up for me. It is empty!

"Oh dear!" says Mrs. Tallyhoo. "How on earth did that get here?"

"I believe it was driven by a certain—"

"CRACKERS!" cries Belinda Bundy.

Snuggled under the leaves, tucked away in a shady corner, is our class hamster. Belinda hands Rin Tin Robot over to me and scoops him up. We thank Mrs. Tallyhoo and hurry back to room 12. Case solved!

CHAPTER 8

FIRST
PRIZE

IT'S THURSDAY night. Time for the science fair. I don't even care who wins. I am just relieved to have another case solved. I did not let my class down!

My whole family walks around the gym. "All these inventions and presentations look amazing," says my father. "I am very proud of you, Walia. You too, Raafe." We smile while Mom tries a piece of fresh cucumber plucked from a third grader's display garden.

When the lights flicker, we know it's time for prizes.

"We have had a lot of drama, indeed—a lot of drama," says Mr. Fussbudget to the audience of lower grade students and their families. His glasses are on crooked and so is his tie. "But still it was a fine showing. Now it is time to reward some truly exceptional work."

He begins shuffling papers, then they fall

to the floor. Two more teachers go over to help. They pick up the papers, but they fall again. The parents seem concerned, but the kids try not to laugh. We're used to Mr. Fuss-budget.

"Thank you, Wednesday." A voice comes at me from the semidarkness. I am surprised to find Anita B. looking at me. "You found my robot. And now we're totally going to win!"

I smile. "I hope you do, Anita B.," I say.

She moves closer and holds out her hand. Even though the lights are low, I see something shiny in her palm. It's the pin!

Silently, she pins the tiny magnifying glass to my sweater.

"Thank you," I say. "But you really don't have to give it to me."

Her face is very serious. "A deal is a deal, Wednesday Walia Nadir. You know that!"

Just then, everyone starts looking in our direction.

". . . and in second place, from Mrs. Gubbins's class, Anita B. Moozeeer," says Mr. Fussbudget.

All the students from room 12 shout out, "It's Moose-E-A!"

Calvin moves up beside me and my brother, Raafe. His brother, Carter, is with him.

"Congratulations, Anita B.," Calvin says. "Your robot is awesome, no matter who made it."

Anita B. squints at him. She says, "So is yours, Calvin. No matter who wins." Then she smiles and heads onto the stage. Calvin's brother gives him a high five.

Next to me, Belinda Bundy whispers, "Crackers is sleeping comfortably in his pen tonight. I checked on him earlier, and the latch is locked tight!"

Anita B. collects her trophy, and we are still whispering when Mr. Fussbudget says, "Walia? Walia Nadir? Oh dear! Is she here? Did she leave? Someone must find her!"

"Woof!" says my dog.

Daddy says, "That man needs to calm down."

"Honey," Mom says, "they called your name."

"Yes, come on up," says Mr. Fussbudget when his eyes find me. "For solving a tricky mystery *with the scientific method*, Wednesday Walia Nadir and her dog, Woof, win first place in the lower grades science fair!"

I pull Belinda along with me toward the stage. "Come with me," I say, and Belinda Bundy takes teeny-tiny hops next to me.

Onstage, I look out over the gym. My parents are applauding. So is Mrs. Gubbins. Mr. Fussbudget mops his brow with a handkerchief.

My insides no longer feel slippery. And my nerves are not buzzing in my ears. We solved the case. Together. Me and my best friend.

And my assistant.

"Woof!"

MYSTERY SOLVED!

CONGRATULATIONS!

You've read **8** chapters,

87 pages,

and **5,391** words!

What a *paw*-some effort!

My hypothesis is that you really enjoy reading mysteries!

What will you read next?

Woof! WOOF!

FUN AND GAMES FOR DETECTIVES IN TRAINING

THINK

In this book, Wednesday uses the scientific method to help solve the case. Try using the scientific method on page 49 to figure out how many drops of water fit onto a nickel. All you need are an eye dropper, a cup of water, and a nickel!

FEEL

In this story, Wednesday feels a lot of pressure to find Anita B.'s robot and Crackers. And Calvin and Anita B. feel a lot of pressure to win the science fair! Draw a picture of a time when you felt stressed out. What helped you feel better?

ACT

Design your own robot using only supplies from the recycling bin. What will it look like? What will you use to make it?

My name is **SHERRI WINSTON**. I grew up in Muskegon Heights, Michigan, where there are lots of lakes and parks and beaches. My favorite color is pink and my favorite books are filled with mystery and adventure. I can't wait to share more stories with you guys, my new friends.

Courtesy of Sherri Winston

My name is **GLADYS JOSE**. I grew up in Orlando, Florida, where each summer my friends and I had adventures pretending we were secret agents. Now I create art every day, with the help of my four-year-old daughter, who has taken on the role of art director, a.k.a. she tells me when I need to redraw something.

Illustration by Gladys Jose